Pumpkins are rich in vitamin A, potassium, and fiber.

October is National Pumpkin Month.

Illinois is the state that grows the most pumpkins.

The first pumpkins grew in Central America.

Things pumpkins make: pies, cookies, breads, soups, muffins, jack o' lanterns, and more.

Native Americans used pumpkin seeds for medicine and food.

Pumpkins are part of the squash family.

Baby Boo, Cinderella, Atlantic Giants, and Jack-Be-Quick are the names of different kinds of pumpkins.

American colonists filled a hollowed pumpkin shell with milk, honey, pumpkin pulp, and spices. They baked it and called it pumpkin pie.

The first jack-o-lanterns were carved out of turnips in Ireland!

Pumpkin Countdown

Joan Holub   Illustrated by Jan Smith

Albert Whitman & Company, Chicago, Illinois

For Kathy, Abby, Jan, and Erin with many thanks.—J.H.

For Sally, Molly, and Mr. B.—J.S.

Library of Congress Cataloging-in-Publication Data

Holub, Joan.
Pumpkin countdown / Joan Holub ; illustrated by Jan Smith.
p. cm.
Summary: When Miss Blue's class visits Farmer Mixenmatch's Pumpkin Patch,
the students find many ways to have fun, and a lot of things to count.
ISBN 978-0-8075-6660-2 (hardcover)
[1. School field trips—Fiction. 2. Farms—Fiction. 3. Pumpkins—Fiction.
4. Counting—Fiction.] I. Smith, Jan, ill. II. Title.
PZ7.H7427Pum 2012 [E]—dc23 2011035889

The design is by Carol Gildar.

For more information about Albert Whitman,
Please visit our web site at www.albertwhitman.com

"It's our pumpkin patch field trip!" shouts Chip.
"Yippee!" says Kiri.
"Woo hoo!" says Drew.

"There are **twenty** nametags to make," says Jake.

"For **nineteen** kids plus Ms. Blue," says Drew.

"**Eighteen** kids get on our bus," says Russ.
"But someone's late," says Kate.
"Wait for me!" calls Kiri.

"Now all ten seats have two," says Drew.
"Okay! We can go!" shouts Ignacio.

"I spy **seventeen** orange things that are not your name tags.
Can you spy them all?" asks Paul.

ANSWERS: Heart on totebag, hair tie, thermal vest, an orange sign, sticker on shirt, a pencil,
a bracelet, a barrette, Claire's hair, star on hoodie, t-shirt, watch, notebook, a ruler, orange flower on backpack,
and a teddy bear key chain.

"Guess **sixteen** things we'll see on our field trip today," says Mei.

"Look! **Fifteen** Pumpkin Street," reads Pete.

"**Fourteen** cars got here before us," says Russ.
"I hope the pumpkins aren't all gone," says Shawn.

"**Thirteen** pumpkins point the way," says Mei.

"Welcome to my Pumpkin Patch!"
calls Farmer Mixenmatch.

"**Twelve** pets in the petting zoo," says Drew.
"Six chicks—four yellow, two black," says Zack.
"Three pigs—two big, one small," says Paul.
"Two goats and one bunny," says Sunny.

"The bunny hopped away!" says Mei.
"But a pony galloped in," says Gwen.
"Still twelve pets in the zoo!" counts Drew.

"Look how a pumpkin grows," says Rose.

"This maze has **ten** scarecrows," says Rose.
"Dead end. Uh-oh!" calls Ignacio.

THE BUZZ ON BEES
Bees get two things from flowers:
1. Nectar to make honey
2. Pollen to eat

"**Eleven** bees are making honey!" says Sunny.

"This way!" calls Mei.
"Come on," calls Shawn.

"Yay! A tractor ride," says Clyde.
"We sit **nine** on each side."
"Plus two in the back," says Zack.

"It's picking time in the pumpkin patch!"
calls Farmer Mixenmatch.

"Wow! Pumpkins everywhere!"
shouts Claire.

"Eight
orange pumpkins, tall,"
says Paul.

Seven yellow
pumpkins, bumpy.

Six pumpkins, green and white.

Lots that are just right!

5 **4**

"**Five** tables, times **four** snacks," says Max.

"**Three** bites. Bye, pumpkin pie!" says Di.

Fairytale

Lumina

Jack-be-quick

Spooktacular

Eastern Rise

Atlantic Giant

"Here's our bus again," says Gwen.
"Buddies line up **two** by **two**," says Drew.
"Back to school we go," says Ignacio.

Ms. Blue knows **one** pumpkin song.
On our bus trip home, we sing along.

Twenty pumpkin pies on the wall.
Twenty pumpkin pies.
Take one down, pass it around.
Nineteen pumpkin pies on the wall . . .

Nineteen pumpkin pies on the wall . . .
Nineteen pumpkin pies.
Take one down, pass it around.
Eighteen pumpkin pies on the wall . . .

We had fun at
the pumpkin patch.
Thanks,
Farmer Mixenmatch!

From Ms. Blue's class

A pumpkin is a fruit.

One pumpkin seed grows one vine.

Pumpkins float because they are 90 percent water.

Pumpkins grow on vines on the ground.

A pumpkin is ready to pick after about four months of growing.

A pumpkin vine can grow up to thirty feet long.

One vine usually grows two to five pumpkins.

Atlantic Giants are some of the biggest pumpkins. One weighed over 1,800 pounds!

A yellow pumpkin flower opens for one day and dies that night. Then a pumpkin starts to grow where the flower was.

A vine's big leaves shade its pumpkins from the hot sun, like umbrellas.